MOTHER GOOSE PAPERCRAFTS

Written and illustrated by

Jerome C. Brown

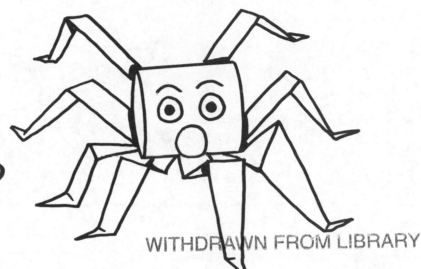

Fearon Teacher Aids
Simon & Schuster Supplementary Education Group

ISBN 0-8224-3154-8
Printed in the United States of America

1.9 8 7 6 5 4 3

CONTENTS

INTRODUCTION

This book contains directions and patterns for making puppets, masks, and other 3-dimensional art projects to enhance the enjoyment of Mother Goose nursery rhymes.

Organizational Helps

Construction paper is used in each papercraft. It is referred to as art paper in the list of materials that accompanies each project. Colors of art paper are suggested but can be changed to suit your needs. Since you will need a pencil, ruler, scissors, glue, and markers or crayons for each project, these items are not listed in each materials list.

For each art project children enjoy, the teacher must spend time in preparation and gathering supplies. This book was designed to minimize that time. Masks are the most common papercraft in this book. A special instruction sheet for this project has been included at the beginning. Once students have mastered the basic format, projects will take less time and explanation. Whole sheets [12" x 18" (30.5 cm x 45.7 cm)], half sheets [9" x 12" (22.9 cm x 30.5 cm)], and quarter sheets [6" x 9" (15.2 cm x 22.9 cm)] of art paper are used whenever possible. This will cut down on the time spent measuring and cutting.

Before beginning each project, reproduce a pattern sheet for each student. Have them cut out all pieces so they can be used for tracing on the colored art paper. For younger children, patterns (which are not cut on a fold line) can be reproduced on white art paper. Color the patterns with markers or crayons and cut them out. This will eliminate the extra steps of tracing and cutting a second time.

Uses for Papercrafts

A coloring page is the first activity listed for each rhyme. Have the children staple each of the coloring pages, followed by a sheet of lined writing paper, together in a book. Have them copy down the rhyme if it is fairly short, or have them make a list of rhyming words. Some children may even enjoy creating a rhyme of their own!

Display the projects on a mural or bulletin board. Let the students create a background with chalk or paint .

Some projects are suitable to be used as props for skits or plays. Allow children the opportunity to reenact the rhyme using their papercraft project.

It is the author's hope that these papercrafts will allow you to bring literature to life in your classroom.

Mask Heads and Puppet Body

Mask Heads:

Fold paper for head and neck lengthwise (fig. A). Use color listed on project page. Trace and cut out two heads and two 1" x 10" (2.5 cm x 25.4 cm) neck strips (fig. B). Be sure to trace eye holes also. Leave head folded and cut out eye holes. Cut through dotted line to make cutting the small hole easier (fig. C). To make neck, cover 1" x 10" (2.5 cm x 25.4 cm) cardboard strip with art paper strips. Glue neck between the two heads allowing 6" (15.2 cm) to extend (fig. D).

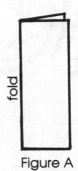

Figure A

Figure B

Figure C

Figure D

Puppet Body:

The puppet body is made with a 12" x 18" (30.5 cm x 45.7 cm) piece of art paper.

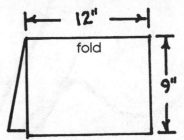

Fold 12" x 18" (30.5 cm x 45.7 cm) into 12" x 9" (30.5 cm x 22.9 cm).

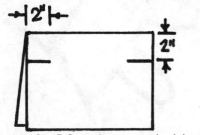

Cut in 2" (5.0 cm) on each side (2" (5.0 cm) from top).

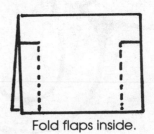

Fold flaps inside.

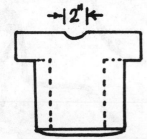

Cut neck hole and insert head.

Hey, Diddle, Diddle

Mother Goose Papercrafts © 1989

Hey, Diddle, Diddle
(The Dish Ran Away with
the Spoon Scene)

Materials

- Four plastic eyes
- 7" (17.8 cm) paper plate
- Plastic spoon
- Patterns on page 8 reproduced on white art paper. (You will need one pattern page for each character.)
- Blue 12" x 18" (30.5 cm x 45.7 cm) art paper for background

Procedure

1. Color and cut out pattern pieces.
2. Using markers or crayons, draw scenery on the blue background paper.
3. Glue plate, spoon, and pattern pieces on background (fig. A).
4. Glue plastic eyes on plate and spoon.
5. Add face details with markers or crayons.

Figure A

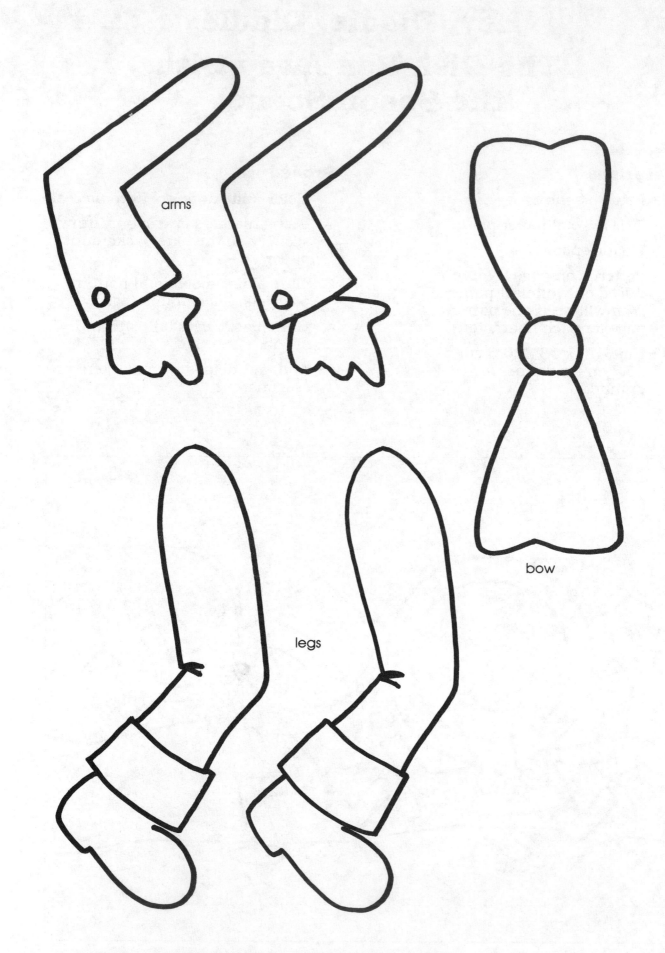

arms

bow

legs

Hey, Diddle, Diddle (Envelope Puppet)

1. Color with markers or crayons.
2. Cut out and glue on a 6" x 9" (15.2 cm x 22.9 cm) manila envelope.
3. Cut off envelope flap.

Humpty Dumpty

Humpty Dumpty Mask

Figure A

Materials

- One 1" x 10" (2.5 cm x 25.4 cm) cardboard strip
- Red chalk or crayon

Art Paper:

- 2 White 12" x 18" (30.5 cm x 45.7 cm) egg heads, neck
- Black 6" x 9" (15.2 cm x 22.9 cm) arms, legs
- Pink 3" x 9" (7.6 cm x 22. 9 cm) collar
- Red 3" x 9" (7.6 cm x 22.9 cm) bow tie

Procedure

1. Follow directions on the top of page 5 for tracing, cutting and gluing head and cardboard neck strip.
2. Trace and cut out remaining pattern pieces.
3. Glue all pieces in place on mask head (fig. A).
4. Draw cheeks with red crayon or chalk and add other details with markers or crayons.

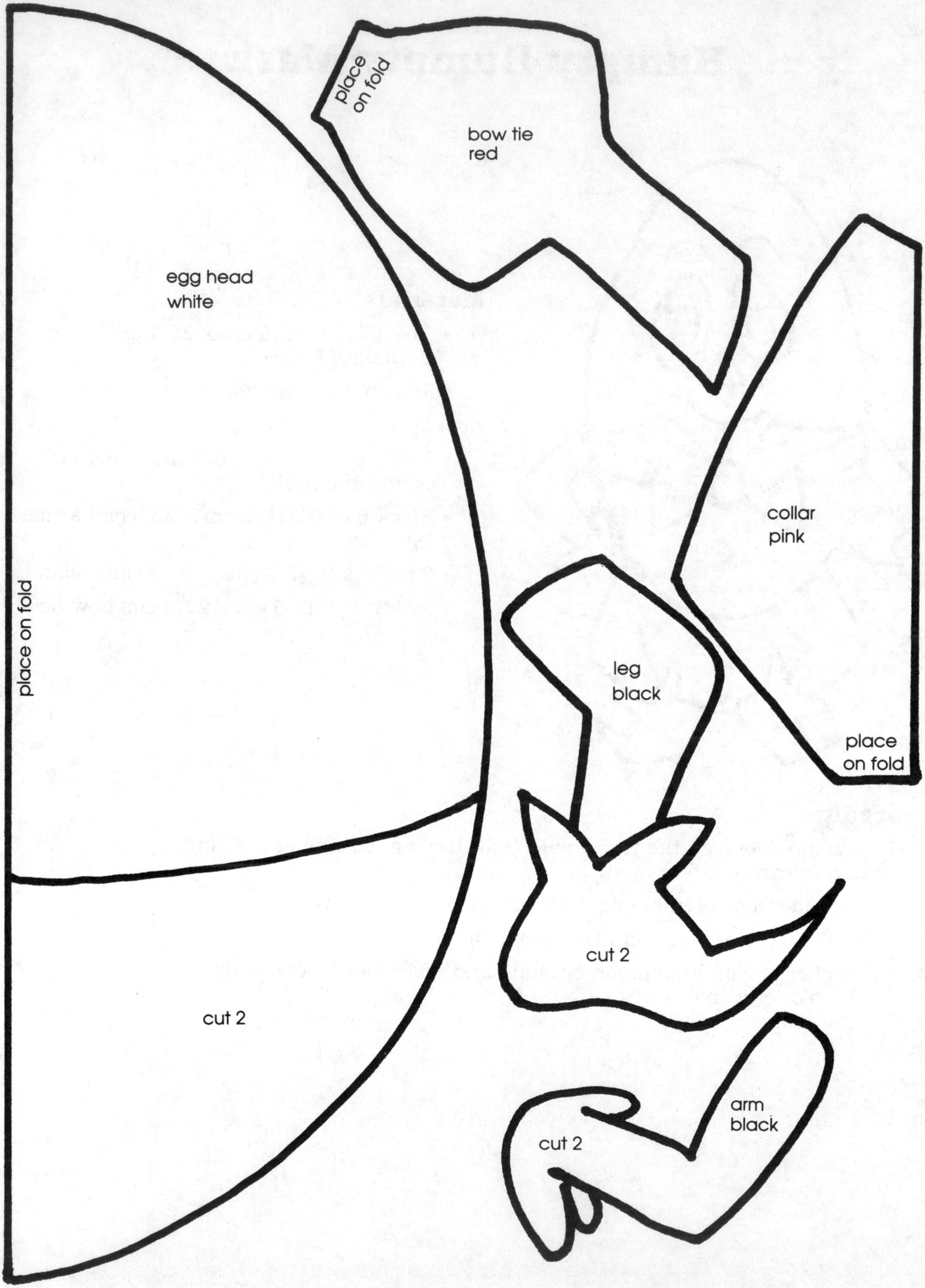

place on fold

bow tie
red

egg head
white

place on fold

collar
pink

place
on fold

leg
black

cut 2

cut 2

arm
black

cut 2

Mother Goose Papercrafts © 1989

Humpty Dumpty Mask

Humpty Dumpty (L'eggs® Puppet)

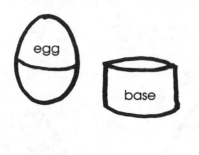

Materials

- L'eggs® egg and cardboard base*
- Two plastic eyes
- Permanent marker

Art Paper:

- 1" x 10" (2.5 cm x 25.4 cm) black strip
- 1" x 10" (2.5 cm x 25.4 cm) orange strip
- Black 2" x 8" (5.0 cm x 20.3 cm) legs
- Orange 2" x 6" (5.0 cm x 15.2 cm) arms
- Scraps of red, pink and white for shoes, tie, nose, hands

Procedure

1. Make a small cut at the top, in the center, of the orange strip and fold it back for a collar (fig. A).
2. Wrap cardboard base with black and orange strips and glue in place (fig. B).
3. Trace and cut out remaining pattern pieces.
4. Glue pieces in place.
5. Glue on plastic eyes and add face details with permanent marker.

*If no base is available, use a strip of cardboard 2" x 11" (5.0 cm x 27.9 cm). Shape it into a cylinder with a 3" (7.6 cm) diameter.

Mother Goose Papercrafts © 1989

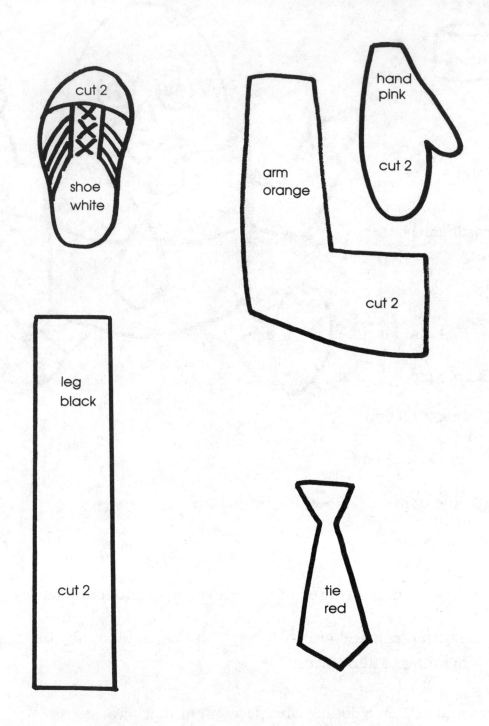

cut 2

shoe
white

hand
pink

arm
orange

cut 2

cut 2

leg
black

cut 2

tie
red

Mother Goose Papercrafts © 1989

Humpty Dumpty (L'eggs ® Puppet)

Jack and Jill

Jack and Jill (Cylinder Puppets)

Materials

- Band-Aid

Art Paper:

- Pink or brown
  9" x 12" (22.9 cm x 30.5 cm) for each body
  3" x 6" (7.6 cm x 15.2 cm) for each pair of hands

- Black 6" x 9" (15.2 cm x 22.9 cm) Jack's pants, hair, shoes

- Yellow 6" x 9" (15.2 cm x 22.9 cm) Jill's hair

- Pink 5" x 6" (12.7 cm x 15.2 cm) Jill's dress

- Red 2" x 4" (5.0 cm x 10.2 cm) Jill's collar

- Blue 5" x 6" (10.2 cm x 15.2 cm) Jack's shirt

Procedure

1. Trace and cut out all pattern pieces.

2. Lay the paper (for the body) flat and glue pieces in place in the center (fig. C). Do not glue down the sleeves of the arms. Allow them to stick out the sides of the puppet.

3. Add details with markers or crayons (figs. A and B).

4. Wait a few minutes for the pieces to dry in place and then shape the paper into a cylinder and staple in the back at the top and bottom.

5. Add Band-Aid to Jack or Jill.

Figure B

Figure C

Mother Goose Papercrafts © 1989

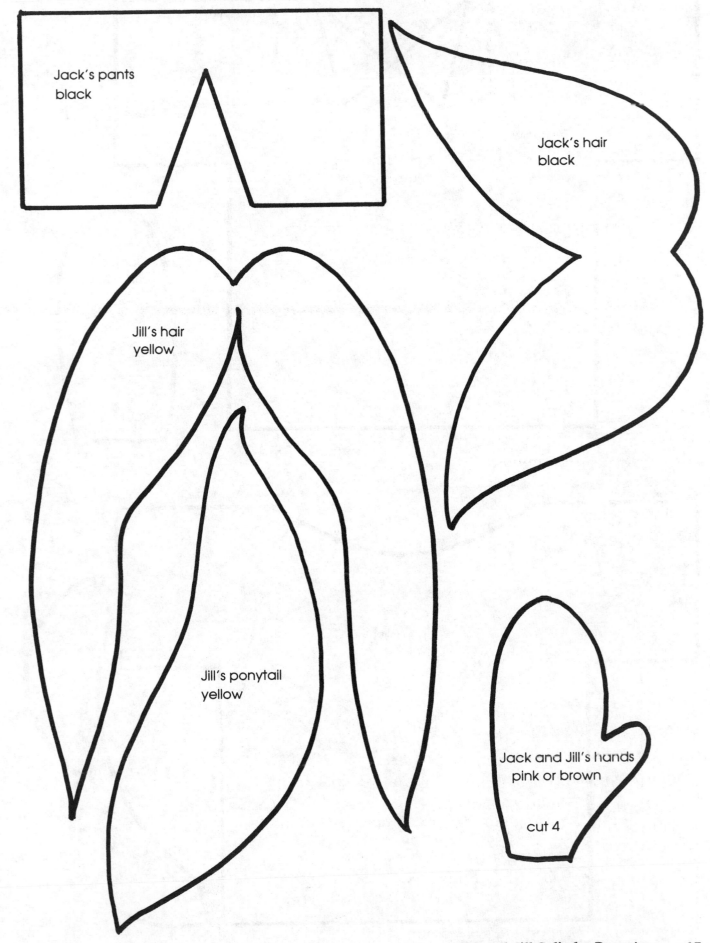

Jack's pants
black

Jack's hair
black

Jill's hair
yellow

Jill's ponytail
yellow

Jack and Jill's hands
pink or brown

cut 4

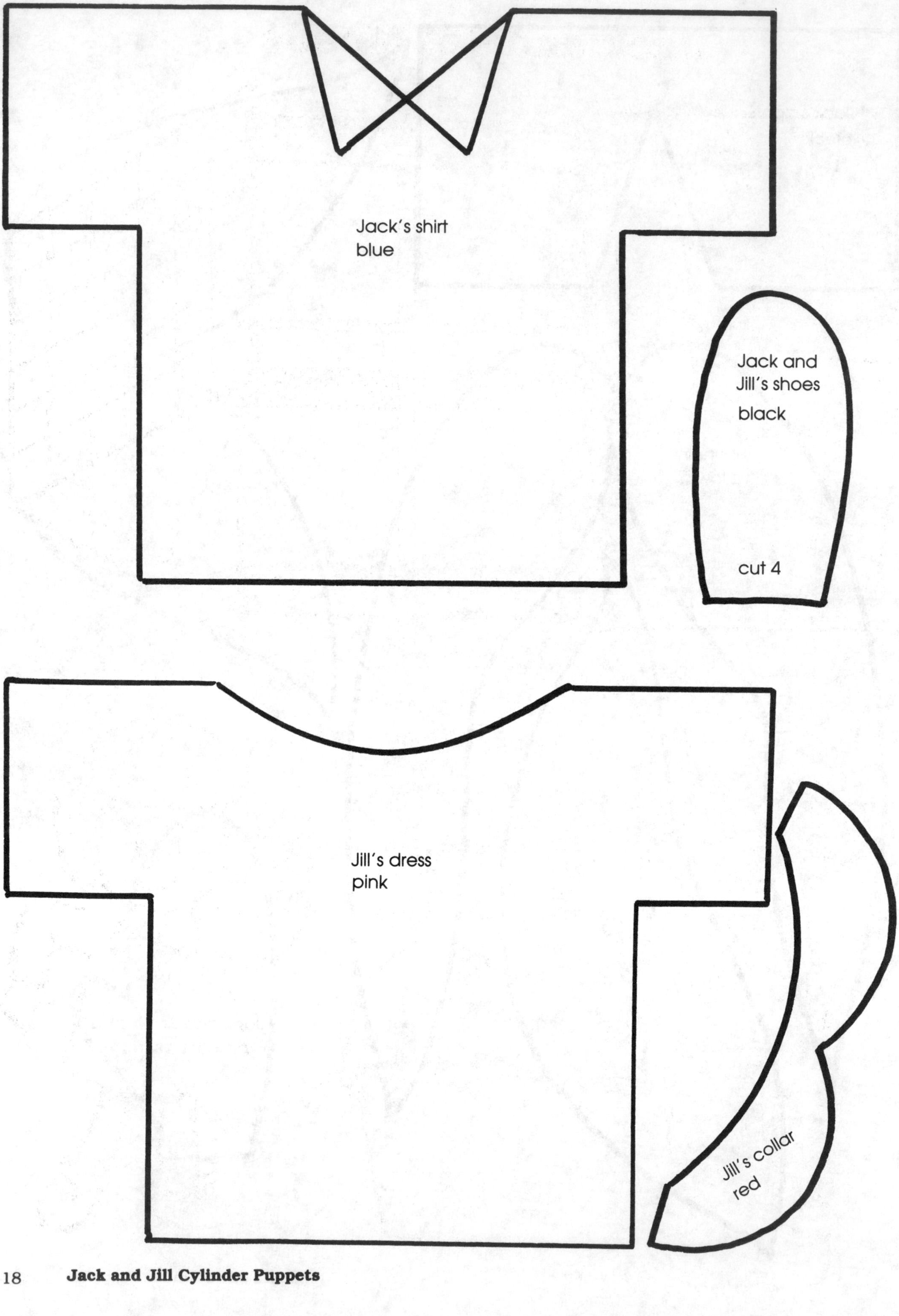

Jack's shirt
blue

Jack and
Jill's shoes
black

cut 4

Jill's dress
pink

Jill's collar
red

Mother Goose Papercrafts © 1989

Jack and Jill Mobile

1. Color figures with markers or crayons and cut them out.

2. Using thread, hang Jack, Jill, and the bucket from the bottom of the well.

Jack Be Nimble

Mother Goose Papercrafts © 1989

Jack Be Nimble (Candlestick)

Materials

- Empty toilet paper roll
- 5" (12.7 cm) aluminum tart pan
- Small piece of aluminum foil

Art Paper:

- Red
  4" x 6" (10.2 cm x 15.2 cm) to
  cover toilet paper roll
  4" x 4" (10.2 cm x 10.2 cm) circle
- White 3" x 6" (7.6 cm x 15.2 cm)
  candle drippings
- Yellow 1" x 2" (2.5 cm x 5.0 cm)
  flame

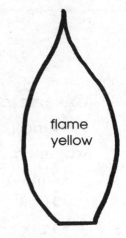

Figure A

staple

Figure B

Procedure

1. Cut 1/2" (1.2 cm) strip off one
   end of toilet paper roll.

2. Cover roll with red paper and glue in place.

3. Trace and cut out candle drippings. Wrap around
   top of roll and glue in place (fig. A).

4. Glue flame to inside of toilet paper roll.

5. Cover 1/2" (1.2 cm) strip with aluminum foil and
   staple on side of tin for handle (fig. B).

6. Using red paper, cut a circle to fit in the bottom of
   the tart pan.

7. Glue candle to red circle as a base and place in
   tart pan.

flame
yellow

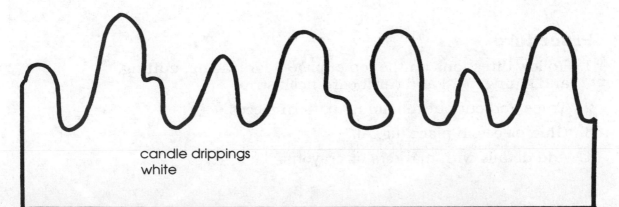

candle drippings
white

Jack Be Nimble Mask

Figure A

Materials

- One 1" x 10" (2.5 cm x 25.4 cm) cardboard strip

Art Paper:

- Pink or brown 12" x 18" (30.5 cm x 45.7 cm) head, neck
- Brown 9" x 12" (22.9 cm x 30.5 cm) hair
- Pink and red scraps

Procedure

1. Follow directions on the top of page 5 for tracing, cutting, and gluing head and cardboard neck strip.

2. Trace and cut out remaining pattern pieces.

3. Glue pieces in place (fig. A).

4. Add details with markers or crayons.

Mother Goose Papercrafts © 1989

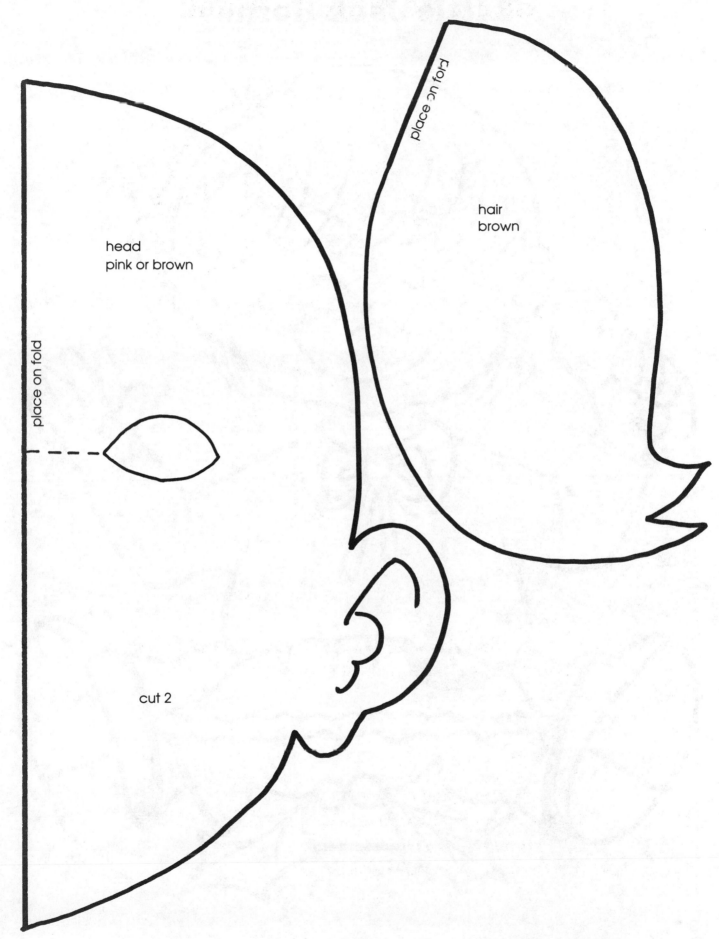

place on fold

head
pink or brown

hair
brown

place on fold

cut 2

Little Jack Horner

Little Jack Horner Puppet

Materials

- One 1" x 10" (2.5 cm x 25.4 cm) cardboard strip
- Aluminum foil 3" x 9" (7.6 cm x 22.9 cm) for pie pan

Art Paper:

- Green 12" x 18" (30.5 cm x 45.7 cm) body
- Pink or brown 12" x 18" (30.5 cm x 45.7 cm) head, neck, hands
- Brown 9" x 12" (22.9 cm x 30.5 cm) hair, pie
- Black 6" x 6" (15.2 cm x 15.2 cm) shoes
- White 3" x 5" (7.6 cm x 12.7 cm) collar
- Purple 2" x 2" (5.0 cm x 5.0 cm) plum shaped oval

Figure A

Procedure

1. Follow directions on page 5 for tracing, cutting, and gluing head and cardboard neck strip and for folding body.

2. Trace and cut out remaining pattern pieces.

3. Glue pieces in place (fig. A).

4. Add details with markers or crayons.

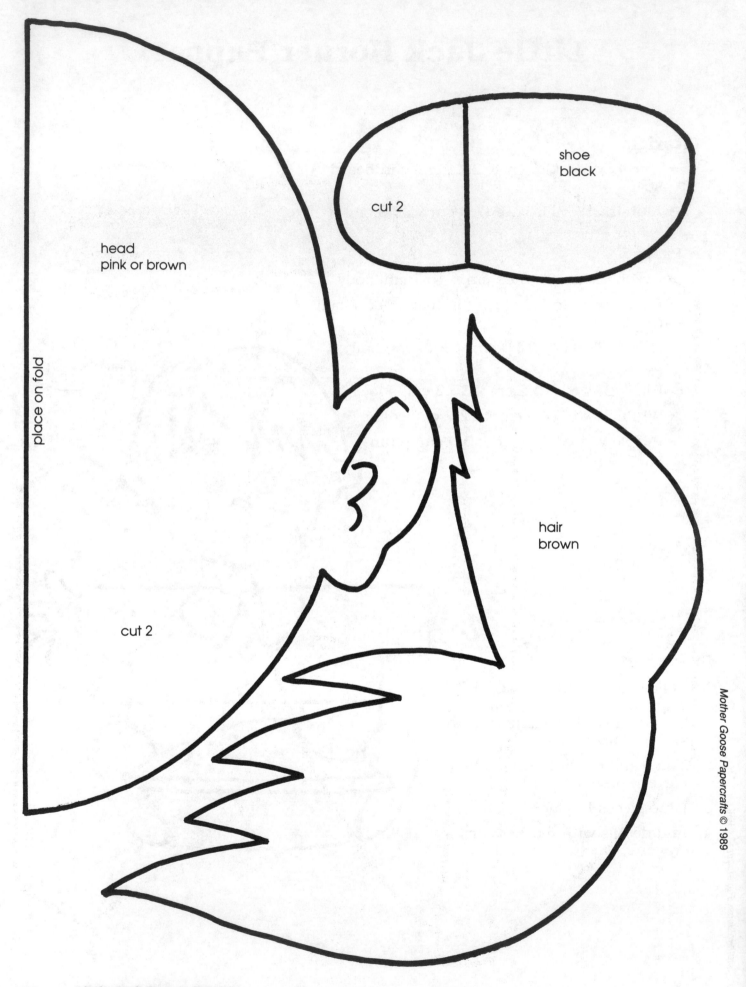

shoe
black

cut 2

head
pink or brown

place on fold

hair
brown

cut 2

Mother Goose Papercrafts © 1989

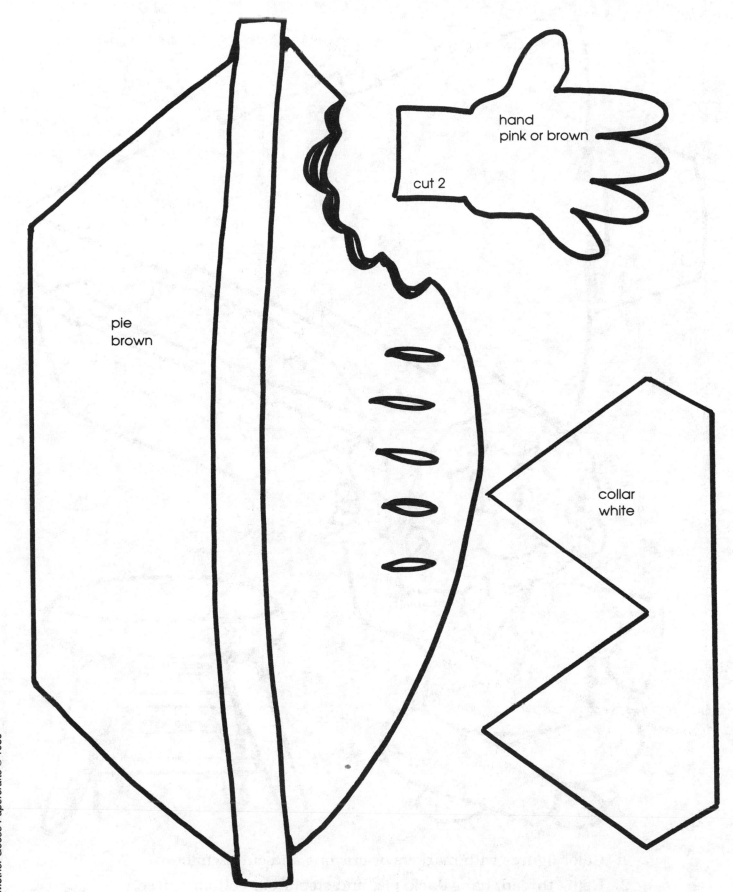

hand
pink or brown

cut 2

pie
brown

collar
white

Little Jack Horner Mobile

Mother Goose Papercrafts © 1989

1. Color figures with markers or crayons and cut them out.
2. Using thread, hang Jack, pie, and stool from bottom of tree.

Little Miss Muffet

Little Miss Muffet Mask

Figure A

Materials

- One 1" x 10" (2.5 cm x 25.4 cm) cardboard strip

Art Paper:

- Pink or brown 12" x 18" (30.5 cm x 45.7 cm) head, neck
- Yellow 9" x 12" (22.9 cm x 30.5 cm) hair (fold lengthwise)

Procedure

1. Follow directions on the top of page 5 for tracing, cutting, and gluing head and cardboard neck strip.
2. Trace and cut out hair patterns.
3. Glue hair in place (fig. A).
4. Add details with markers or crayons.

Mother Goose Papercrafts © 1989

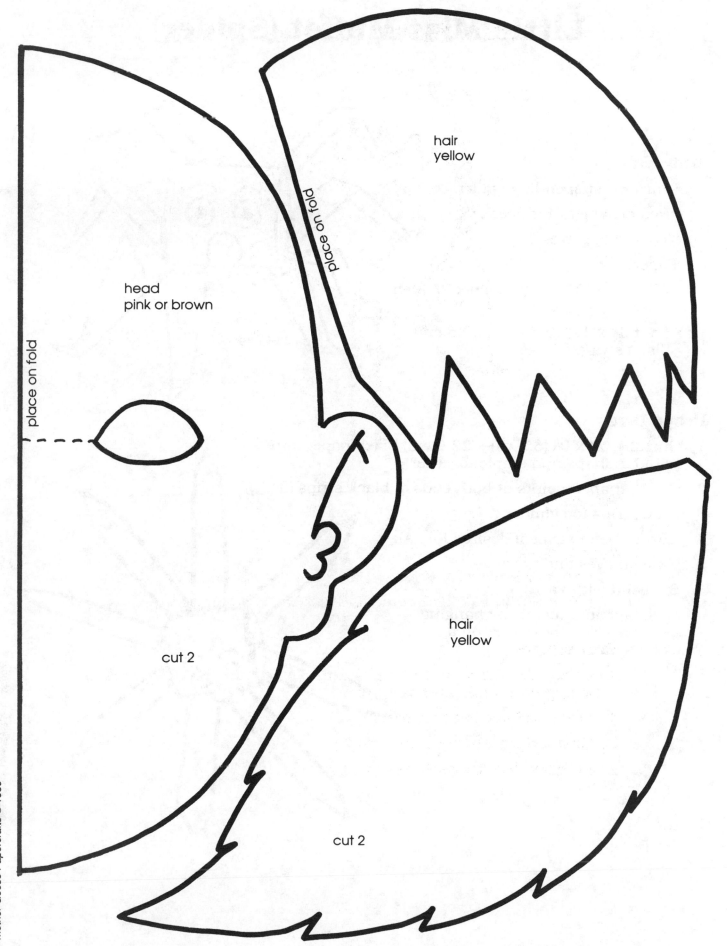

place on fold

head
pink or brown

place on fold

hair
yellow

cut 2

hair
yellow

cut 2

Little Miss Muffet Mask

Little Miss Muffet (Spider)

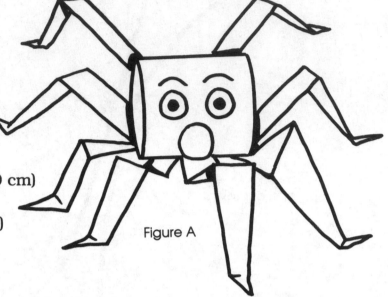

Materials

- Yarn for suspending spider
- Red ornament for nose
- Two plastic eyes

Art Paper:

- Black 2 1/2" x 9" (6.2 cm x 22.9 cm) body
- Four 1" x 12" (2.5 cm x 30.5 cm) black strips

Figure A

Procedure

1. Curl 2 1/2" x 9" (6.2 cm x 22.9 cm) black paper into cylinder shape and staple together.
2. Cut V-shaped points at both ends of black strips (fig. B).
3. Glue strips to cylinder.
4. Curl or bend strips if desired (fig. A).
5. Glue on eyes and nose.
6. Suspend with yarn.

   Make a spider mobile by hanging severals spiders together on a clothes hanger.

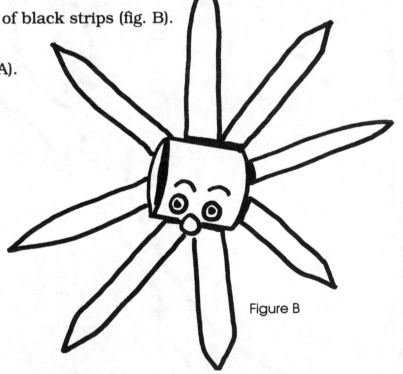

Figure B

Mother Goose Papercrafts © 1989

Mary Had a Little Lamb

Mary Had a Little Lamb (Lamb)

Materials

- 35 small cotton balls
- One plastic eye

Art Paper:

- Black 9" x 12" (22.9 cm x 30.5 cm) lamb body
- Pink scraps for ears and nose

Figure A

Procedure

1. Trace lamb pattern on folded art paper. Cut out.
2. Glue both halves together.
3. Trace and cut out ears and nose.
4. Cover one side of body with cotton balls.
5. Glue on eye, ears, and nose.

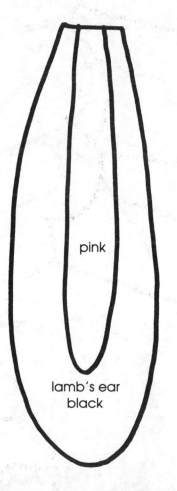

pink

lamb's ear
black

place on fold

Mary Had a Little Lamb (Lamb)   35

Mary Had a Little Lamb
(Envelope Puppet)

Materials

- Manila envelope 6" x 9" (15.2 cm x 22.9 cm)
- Red art paper 6" x 9" (15.2 cm x 22.9 cm) bandana
- Reproduced pattern on page 37

Procedure

1. Color reproduced pattern on page 37 with markers or crayons.
2. Cut the figure out and glue it on manila envelope. Be sure to put the bottom of the figure at the open end of the envelope. Cut off the envelope flap (fig. A).
3. Trace and cut out bandana and glue in place on puppet.

Figure A

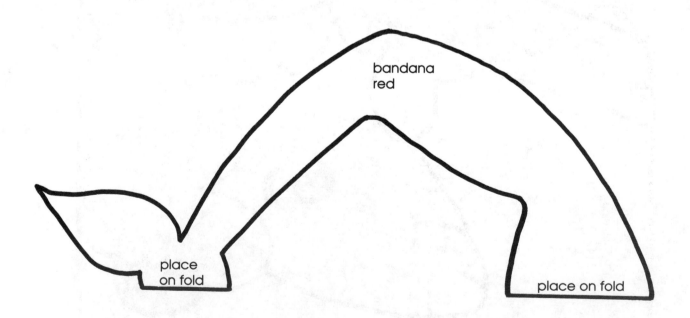

bandana
red

place on fold

place on fold

Mary Had a Little Lamb Envelope Puppet

Mary, Mary Quite Contrary

Mary, Mary Quite Contrary
(Stand-Up Garden)

Materials

Art Paper:

- Blue 9" x 18" (22.9 cm x 45.7 cm) background cylinder
- Pink 6" x 12" (15.2 cm x 30.5 cm) flowers
- Yellow 4 1/2" x 6" (11.4 cm x 15.2 cm) flower centers
- White 6" x 9" (15.2 cm x 22.9 cm) butterflies
- Green 9" x 12" (22.9 cm x 30.5 cm) stems and leaves

Figure A

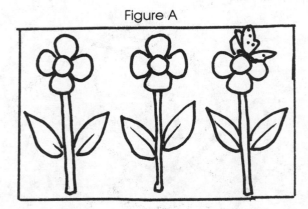

Procedure

1. Trace and cut out all pattern pieces.
2. Lay the blue paper flat on the table. Glue all cut outs in place (fig. A).
3. Add details with markers or crayons.
4. Wait a few minutes for the glue to begin to dry. Shape the blue paper into a cylinder and staple so the garden will stand.

Mother Goose Papercrafts © 1989

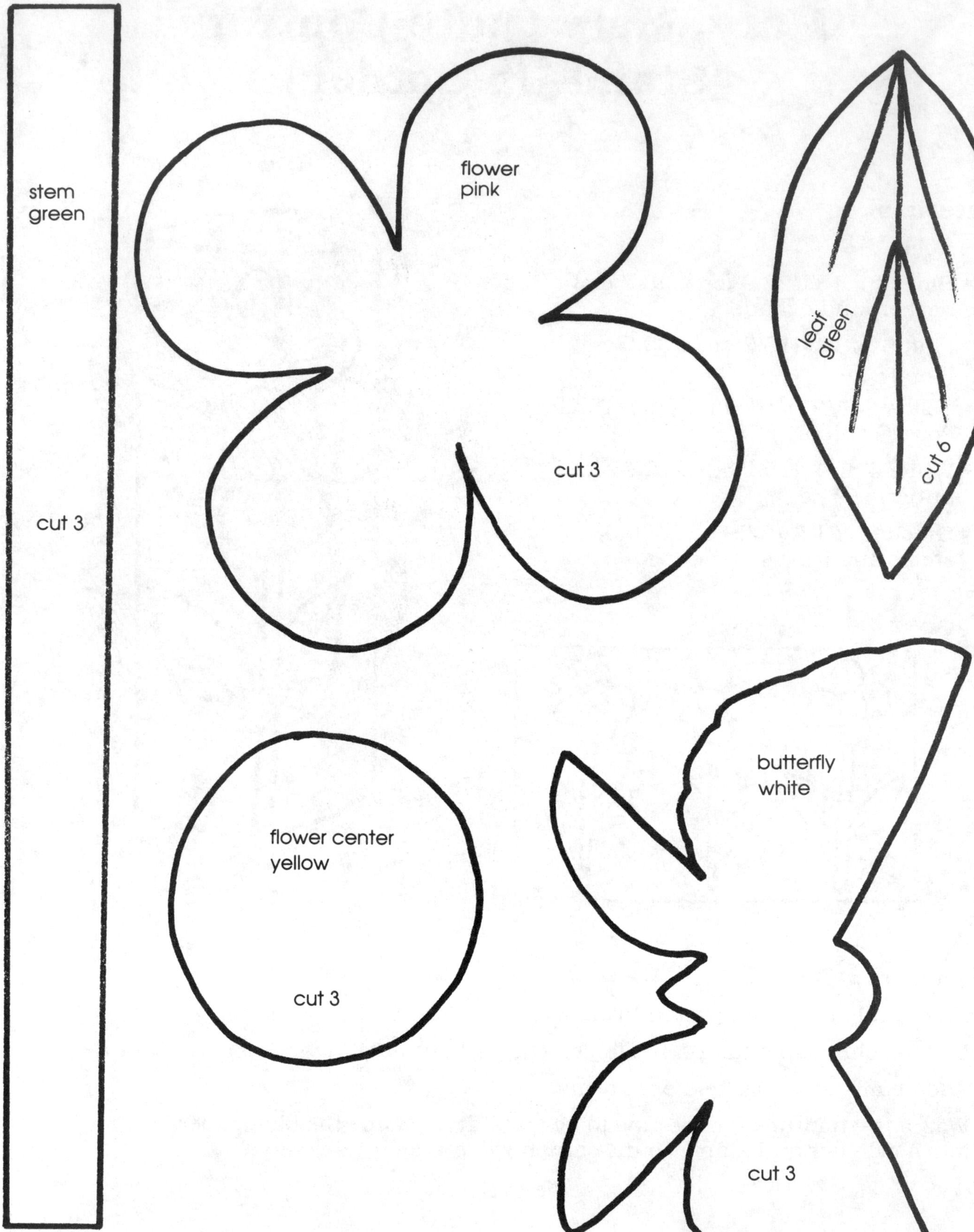

stem
green

cut 3

flower
pink

cut 3

leaf
green

cut 6

flower center
yellow

cut 3

butterfly
white

cut 3

Mary, Mary Quite Contrary (Stand-Up Garden)

Mary, Mary Quite Contrary (Watering Can)

Materials

- Four green pipe cleaners
- Small juice can
- Small ball of clay

Art Paper:

- Purple 3 1/2" x 8" (8.8 cm x 20.3 cm) to wrap juice can (size may vary)
- Purple 6" x 9" (15.2 cm x 22.9 cm) handle, spout
- Green 6" x 9" (15.2 cm x 22.9 cm) leaves
- Yellow 3" x 6" (7.6 cm x 15.2 cm) centers
- Orange 9" x 12" (22.9 cm x 30.5 cm) flowers

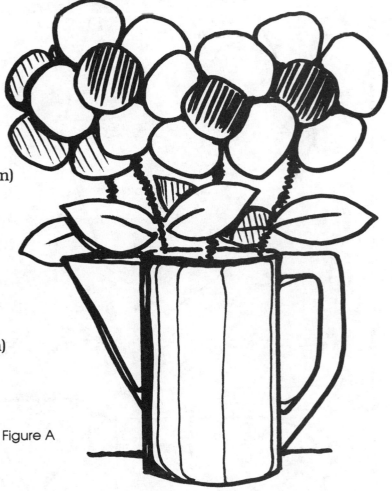

Figure A

Procedure

1. Cover juice can with purple paper.

2. Trace and cut out spout and handle. Fold spout on dotted lines and glue Flaps 1 and 2 together. Fold handle on dotted line and glue together (figs. B and C). Glue spout and handle in the appropriate place on the covered juice can (fig. A).

3. Trace and cut out flowers, centers, and leaves.* Glue a yellow center on each orange flower. Glue a pipe cleaner between two flowers and glue two leaves on the pipe cleaner stem. Repeat with the remaining three flower stems.

4. Put the ball of clay in the bottom of the watering can. Stick the flower stems in the clay to hold them in place.

*To simplify the project, duplicate a page of eight orange flowers and have the students cut them out. Do the same with the yellow centers and green leaves.

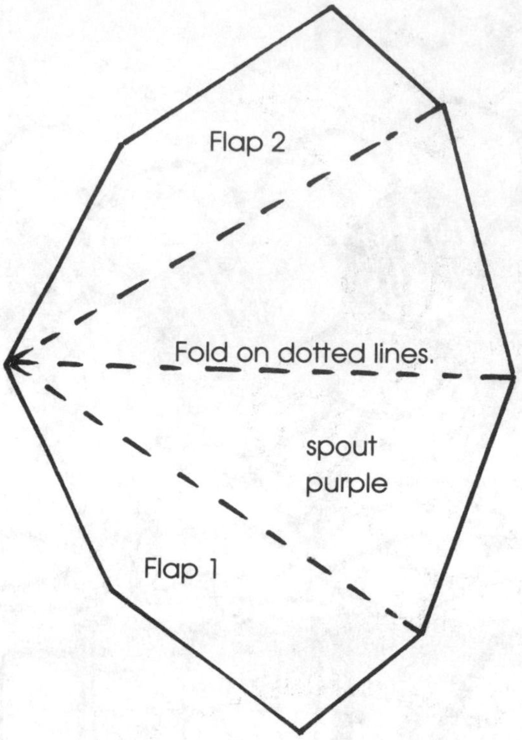

Flap 2

Fold on dotted lines.

spout
purple

Flap 1

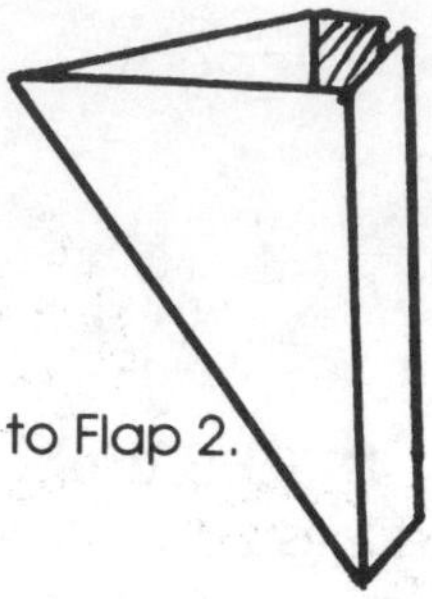

Glue Flap 1 to Flap 2.

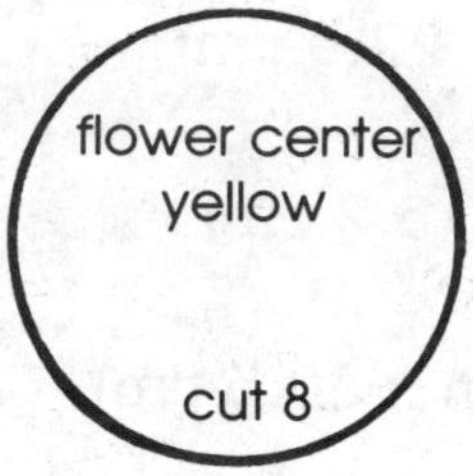

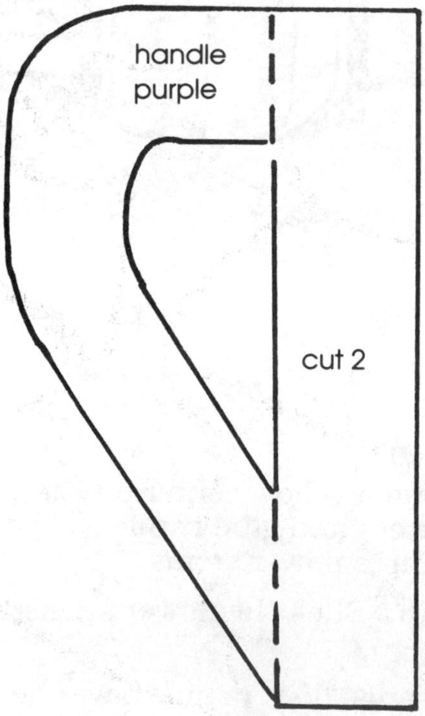

flower center
yellow

cut 8

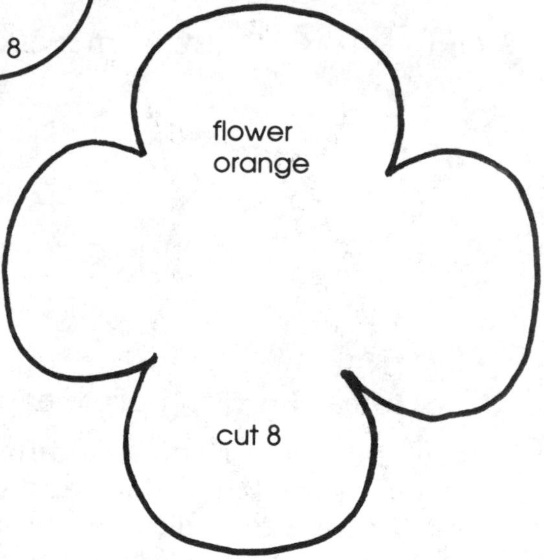

handle
purple

cut 2

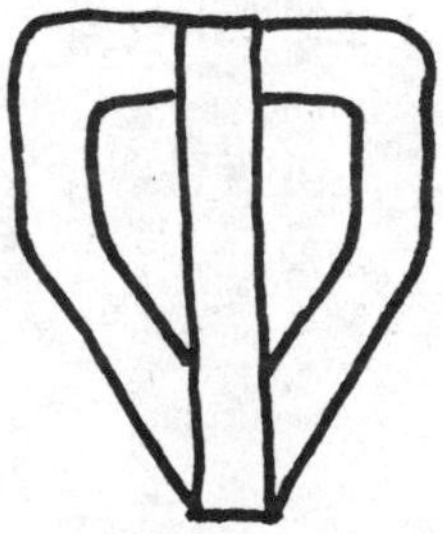

Figure B

Figure C

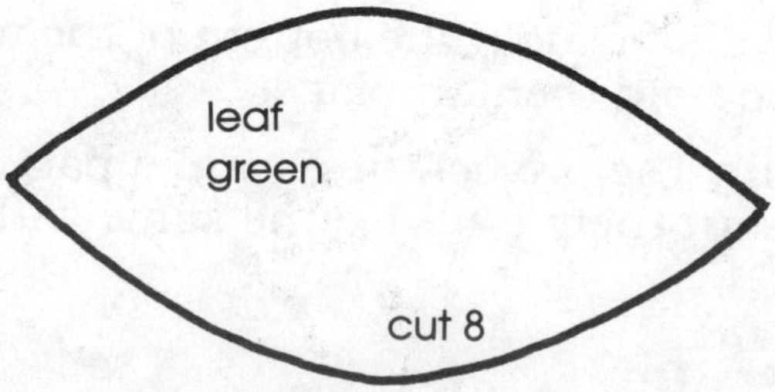

flower
orange

cut 8

leaf
green

cut 8

Mother Goose Papercrafts © 1989

Old King Cole

Old King Cole's Crown

yellow

purple

Figure B

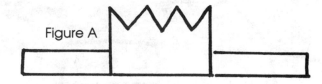

Figure A

Materials

- Glitter

Art Paper:

- Crown pattern on page 45 reproduced on red 9" x 12" (22.9 cm x 30.5 cm) paper
- Two 1 1/2" x 9" (3.7 cm x 22.9 cm) red strips
- Yellow or purple scraps

Procedure

1. Cut out red crown.
2. Staple the red strips to each side of the crown and then make into a circle to fit the child's head and staple (fig. A).
3. Add details with glitter and scraps of yellow or purple paper.

Mother Goose Papercrafts © 1989

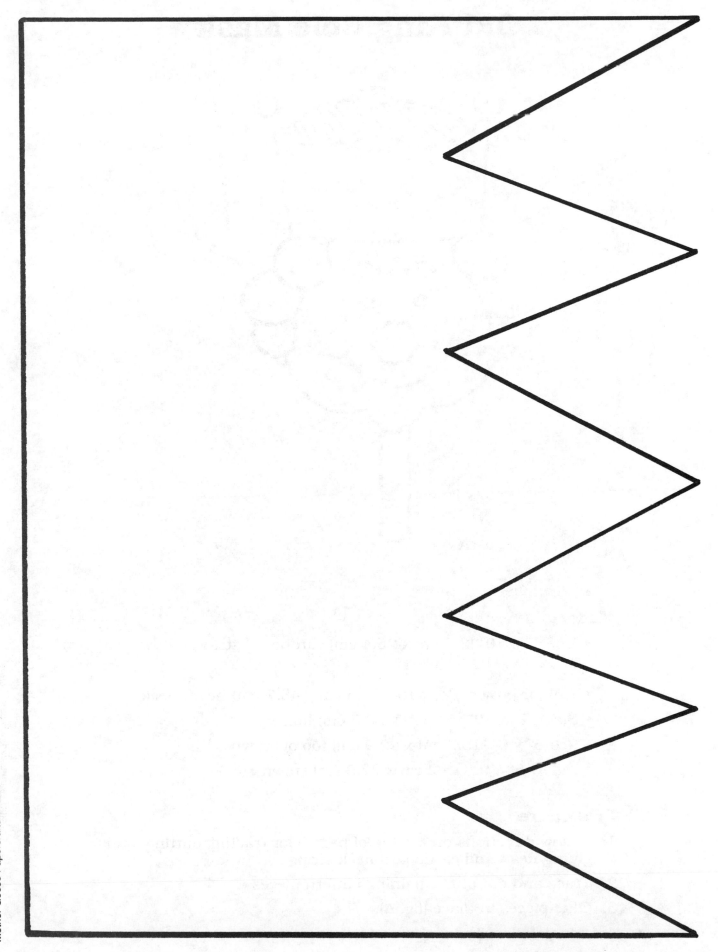

Old King Cole's Crown 45

Old King Cole Mask

Figure A

Materials

- One 1" x 10" (2.5 cm x 25.4 cm) cardboard strip

Art Paper:

- Pink or brown 12" x 18" (30.5 cm x 45.7 cm) head, neck
- Black 2" x 12" (5.0 cm x 30.5 cm) hair
- Red 6" x 9" (15.2 cm x 22.9 cm) top of crown
- Yellow 6" x 9" (15.2 cm x 22.9 cm) crown

Procedure

1. Follow directions on the top of page 5 for tracing, cutting, and gluing head and cardboard neck strip.

2. Trace and cut out remaining pattern pieces.

3. Glue pieces in place (fig. A).

4. Add details with markers or crayons.

Mother Goose Papercrafts © 1989

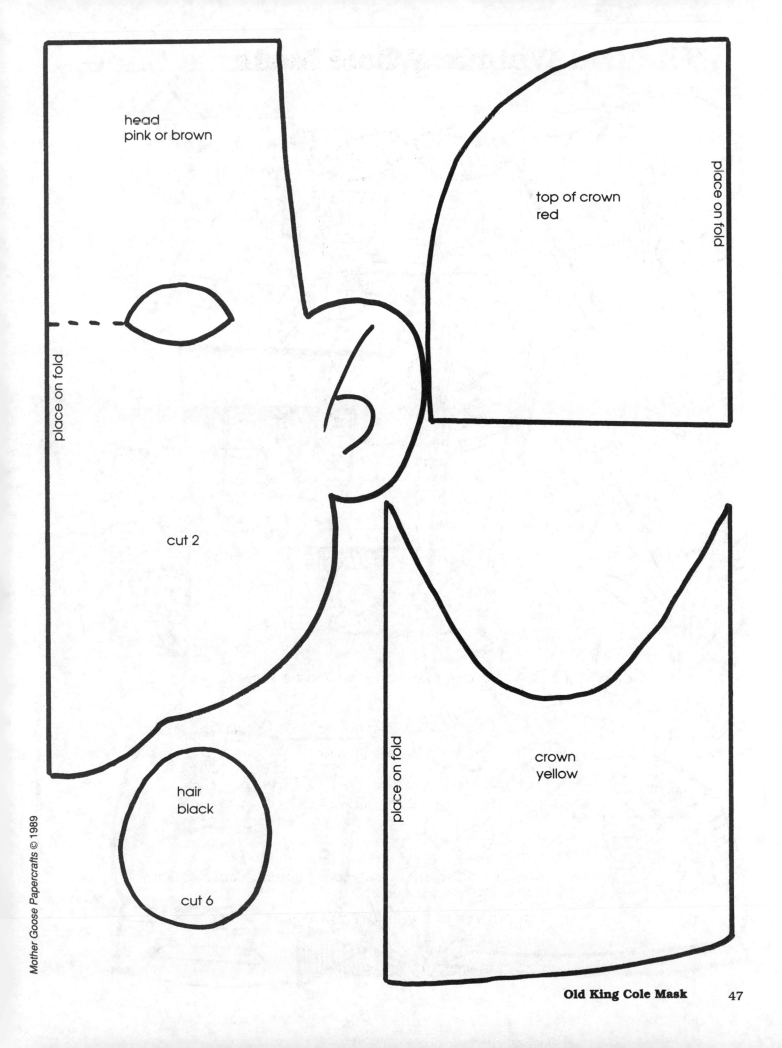

head
pink or brown

place on fold

cut 2

top of crown
red

place on fold

hair
black

cut 6

place on fold

crown
yellow

Mother Goose Papercrafts © 1989

Old King Cole Mask

The Old Woman Who Lived in a Shoe

The Old Woman Who Lived in a Shoe
(3-D Shoe)

Materials

Art Paper:

- Yellow 9" x 12" (22.9 cm x 30.5 cm) shoe
- Red 4" x 4" (10.2 cm x 10.2 cm) roof
- Black 3" x 3" (7.6 cm x 7.6 cm) smokestack

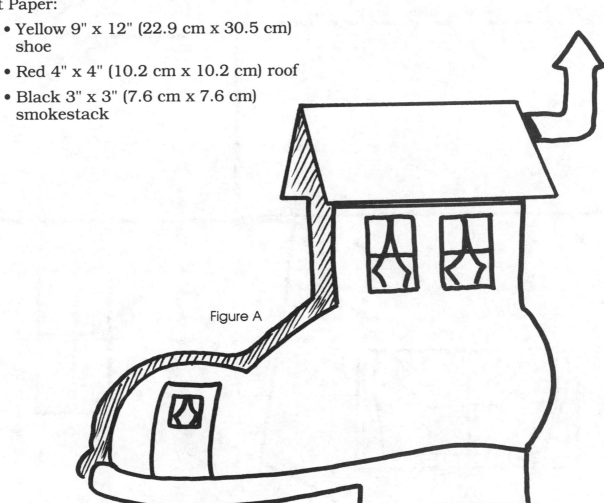

Figure A

Procedure

1. Trace and cut out all pattern pieces.
2. Glue the smokestack between the two shoe pieces and glue the roof in place.
3. Add details with markers or crayons (fig. A).
4. Do not glue the two shoe pieces together. They remain separate to allow the shoe to stand up.

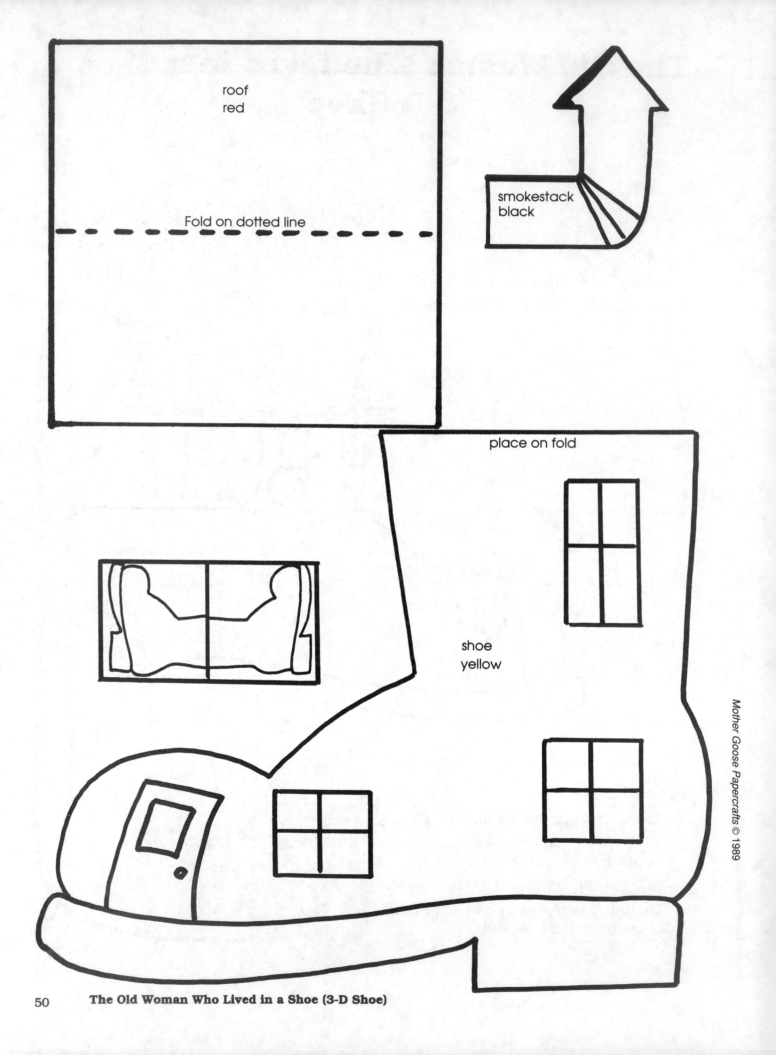

roof
red

Fold on dotted line

smokestack
black

place on fold

shoe
yellow

The Old Woman Who Lived in a Shoe (3-D Shoe)

Mother Goose Papercrafts © 1989

Peter, Peter Pumpkin Eater

Peter Peter Pumpkin Eater Scene

Materials

- Reproduced copy of Peter and his wife
- X-ACTO knife

Art Paper:

- Pumpkin pattern on page 53 reproduced on orange 9" x 12" (22.9 cm x 30.5 cm) paper
- Green 2" x 2" (5.0 cm x 5.0 cm) stem
- Blue 12" x 18" (30.5 cm x 45.7 cm) for background

Procedure

1. Cut out the orange pumpkin.
2. Using the X-ACTO knife, cut out the window on the pumpkin and three sides of the door.
3. Glue green paper over stem of pumpkin and trim around the edges.
4. Color and cut out the figures of Peter and his wife.
5. Glue the wife behind the window so her head shows through.
6. Glue the pumpkin on the blue background paper.
7. Glue Peter in the open doorway.

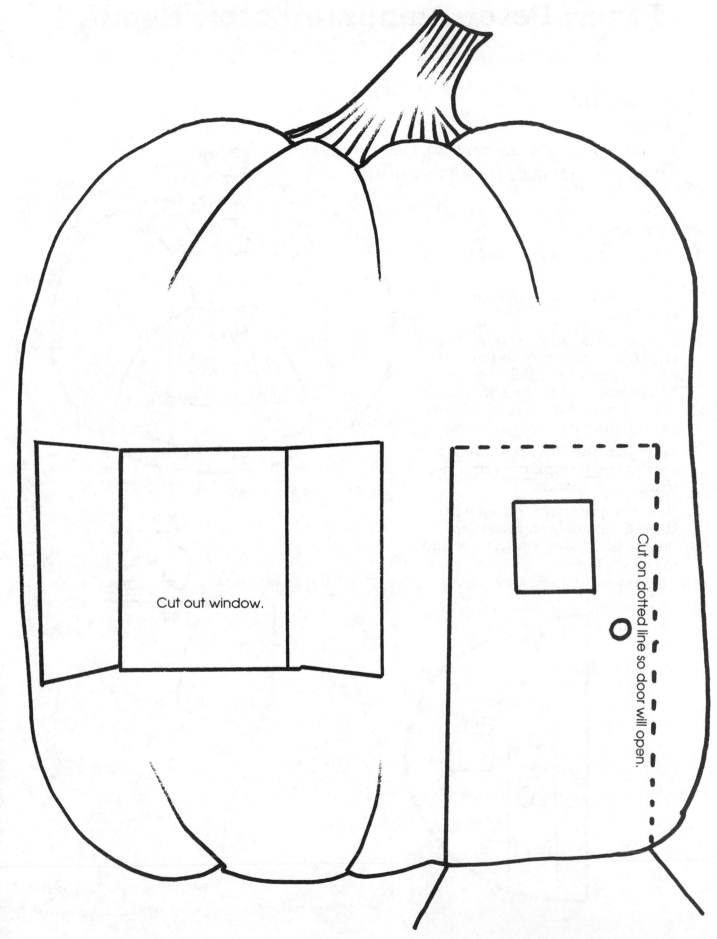

Cut out window.

Cut on dotted line so door will open.

Peter, Peter Pumpkin Eater (Pop-Up)

Materials

Art Paper:

* Orange 9" x 12" (22.9 cm x 30.5 cm) pumpkin
* White 9" x 12" (22.9 cm x 30.5 cm) wife

Procedure

1. Trace and cut out pumpkin and wife patterns.

2. Color the wife with markers or crayons.

3. Fold the wife as shown in Figure B. This step is very important for the wife to actually pop up. When you unfold the wife she should have a V-shaped fold line as in Figure A.

4. Glue just the skirt portion of the wife to the pumpkin so that her head folds forward.

5. Fold the pumpkin in half with the wife inside and draw the door and window on the outside (fig. C).

Figure A

Fold lines are in a V shape.

Figure B

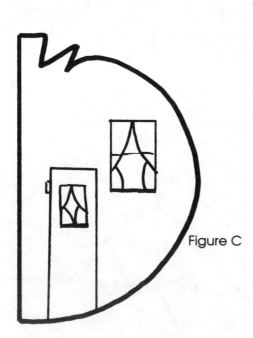

Figure C

Mother Goose Papercrafts © 1989

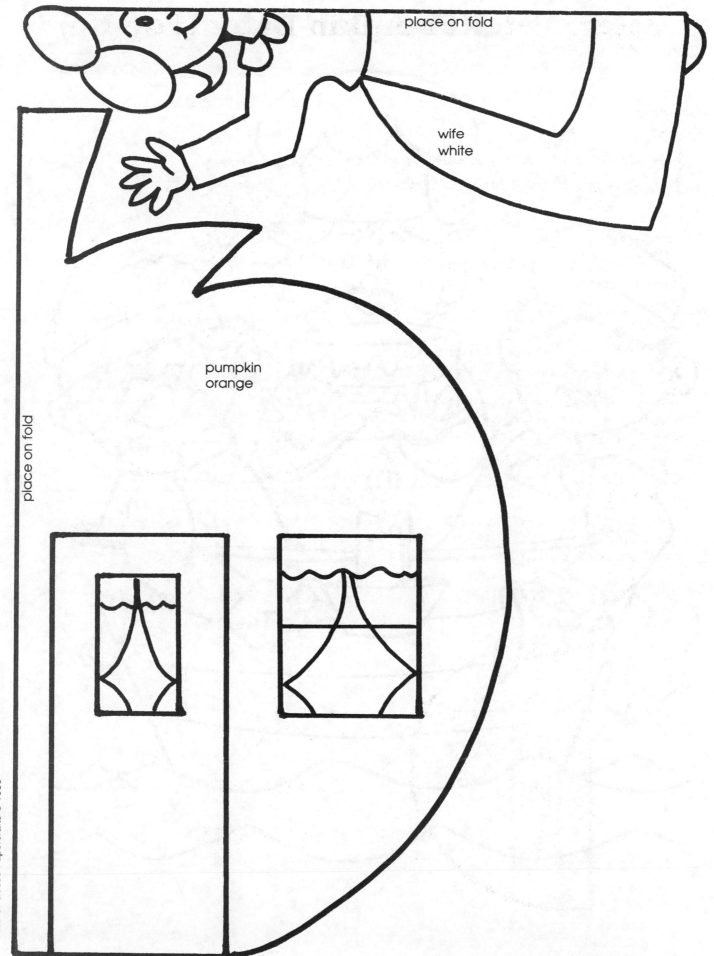

place on fold

wife
white

pumpkin
orange

place on fold

Rub-A-Dub-Dub

Rub-A-Dub-Dub (Cylinder Puppets)

Materials

Art Paper:

- Pink or brown 9" x 12" (22.9 cm x 30.5 cm) for each puppet
- 4 1/2" x 6" (11.4 cm x 15.2 cm) nose, ears for each puppet

Candlestick Maker

- Red 9" x 12" (22.9 cm x 30.5 cm) hat, scarf
- Black 6" x 9" (15.2 cm x 22.9 cm) hair strips, bow

Butcher

- Black 4" x 5" (10.2 cm x 12.7 cm) cap
- Yellow 3" x 6" (7.6 cm x 15.2 cm) bow
- Red 4 1/2" x 6" (11.4 cm x 15.2 cm) side-burns, mustache
- Blue 3" x 9" (7.6 cm x 22.9 cm) scarf

Baker

- White 5" x 5" (12.7 cm x 12.7 cm) hat
- Black 6" x 9" (15.2 cm x 22.9 cm) mustache, hair
- Red 6" x 9" (15.2 cm x 22.9 cm) scarf, bow

Procedure

1. Trace and cut out all patterns.
2. Lay 9" x 12" (22.9 cm x 30.5 cm) pink or brown paper flat on table. Glue pieces in place (figs. A, B, and C). Glue just the end of the ears down so they will stick out when the puppet is completed.
3. Add other details with markers or crayons.
4. Shape paper into a cylinder and staple.

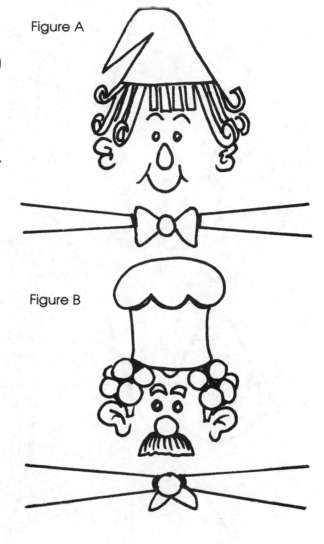

Figure A

Figure B

Figure C

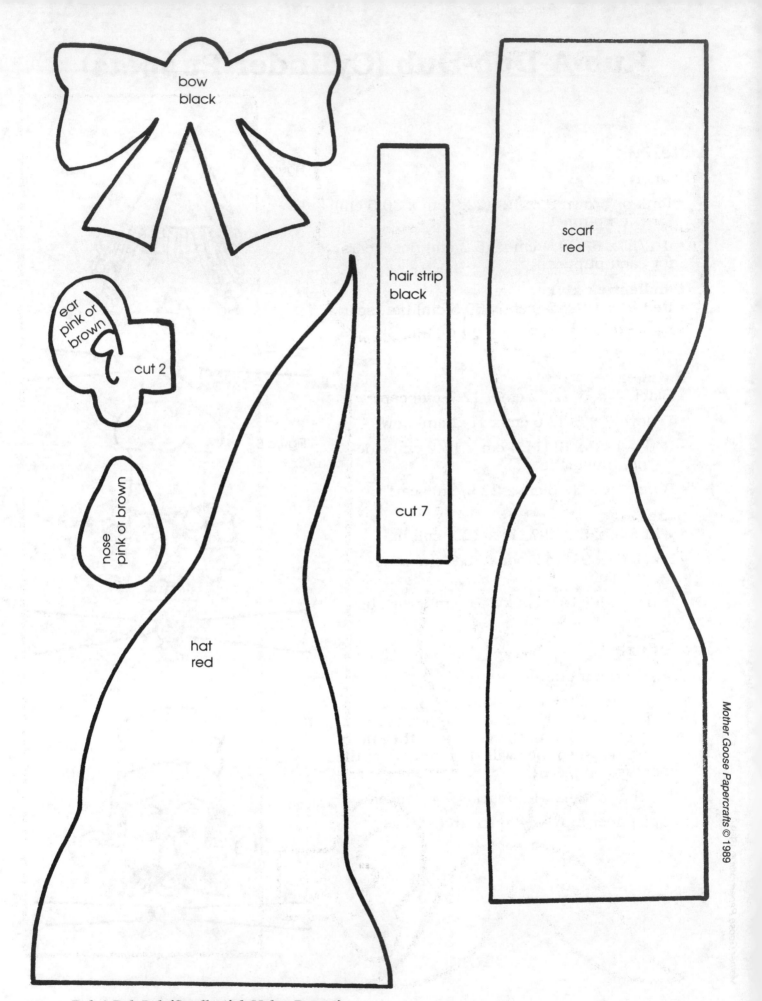

bow
black

ear
pink or
brown

cut 2

nose
pink or brown

hair strip
black

cut 7

scarf
red

hat
red

Rub-A-Dub-Dub (Candlestick Maker Puppet)

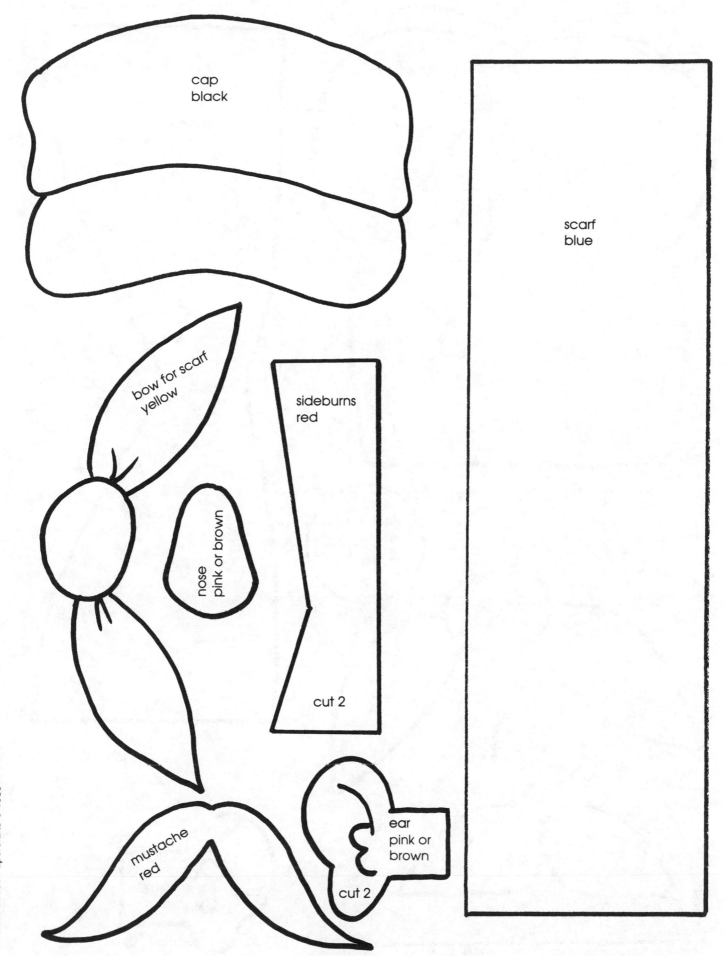

cap
black

scarf
blue

bow for scarf
yellow

sideburns
red

nose
pink or brown

cut 2

mustache
red

ear
pink or
brown

cut 2

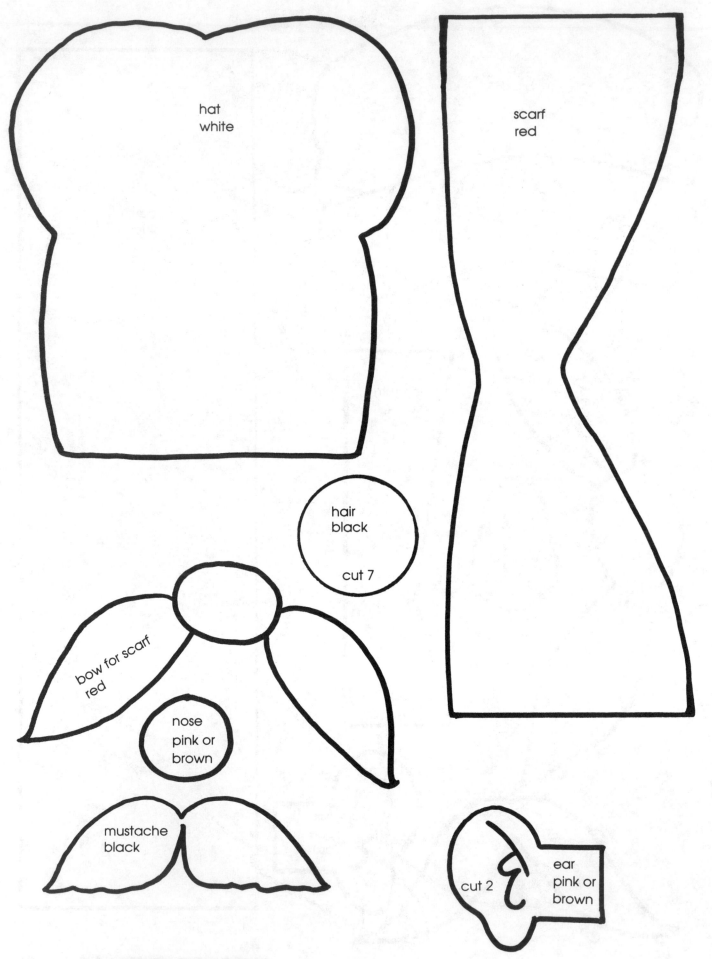

hat
white

scarf
red

hair
black

cut 7

bow for scarf
red

nose
pink or
brown

mustache
black

ear
pink or
brown

cut 2

Mother Goose Papercrafts © 1989

60   **Rub-A-Dub-Dub (Baker Puppet)**

Three Blind Mice

Three Blind Mice (Mouse Mask)

Figure A

Materials

- One 1" x 10" (2.5 cm x 25.4 cm) cardboard strip

Art Paper:

- White 12" x 18" (30.5 cm x 45.7 cm) head, neck
- Black 6" x 9" (15.2 cm x 22.9 cm) glasses, nose
- Pink 6" x 9" (15.2 cm x 22.9 cm) muzzle, ears

Procedure

1. Follow directions on the top of page 5 for tracing, cutting, and gluing head and cardboard neck strip.

2. Trace and cut out remaining pattern pieces.

3. Glue pieces in place (fig. A).

4. Add details with markers or crayons.

Mother Goose Papercrafts © 1989

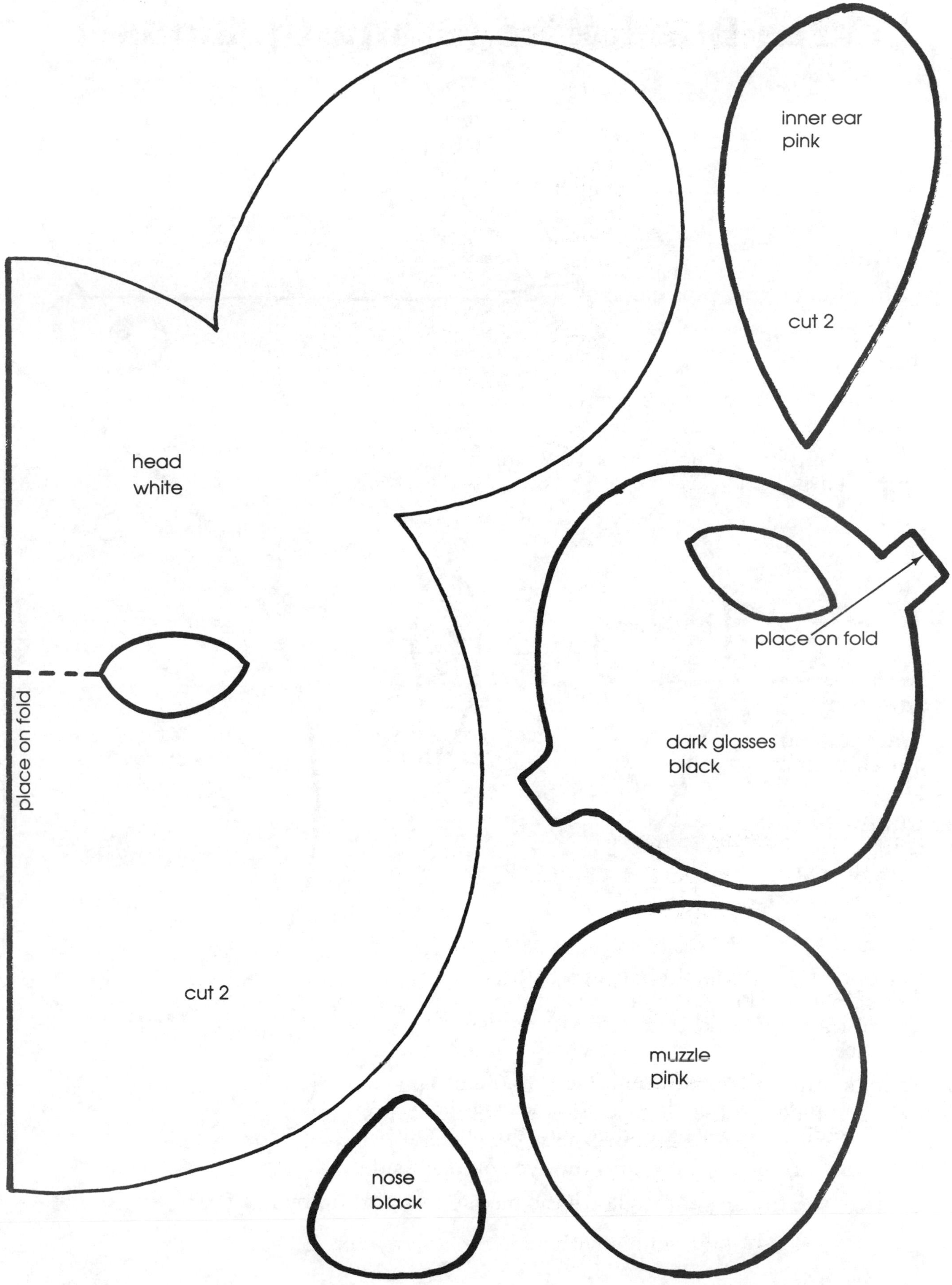

inner ear
pink

cut 2

head
white

place on fold

cut 2

place on fold

dark glasses
black

muzzle
pink

nose
black

Three Blind Mice (Mouse Mask)

Three Blind Mice (Stand-Up Mouse)

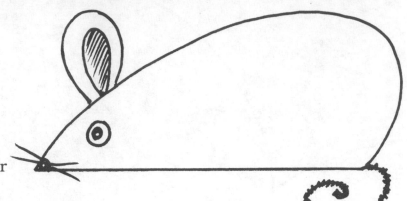

Materials

- One pink or gray pipe cleaner
- Two plastic eyes

Art Paper:

- Pink or gray 9" x 12" (22.9 cm x 30.5 cm) mouse, ear
- Bright pink 2" x 4" (5.0 cm x 10.2 cm) inner ears

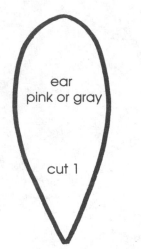

ear
pink or gray

cut 1

inner ear
bright pink

cut 2

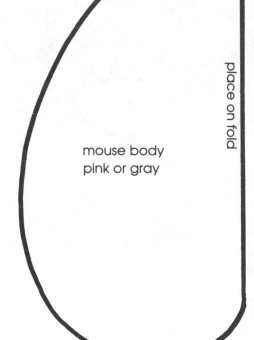

mouse body
pink or gray

place on fold

Procedure

1. Trace and cut out all pattern pieces.

2. Cut two 2" (5.0 cm) pieces of pipe cleaner. The remainder will be used for the tail.

3. Place the tail in the fold between both mouse pieces. Place the outer ear in the appropriate spot and then glue the mouse together.

4. To make the whiskers, push the 2" (5.0 cm) pieces of pipe cleaner through the nose end of the mouse so they extend equally on both sides.

5. Glue the inner ear pieces and the eyes on each side.

6. Arrange the tail so that it allows the mouse to stand up by itself.

Mother Goose Papercrafts © 1989